The Adventures of Paddington™

My Sticky Sticker Book

Paddington is having lots of messy fun with marmalade, ice cream and other sticky treats! Do you know who else likes sticky things? Bees!

Add a sticker here every time you spot a buzzy bee in the book!

HarperCollins *Children's Books*

Time to tuck in

Paddington believes that all of the best days begin with a marmalade sandwich. Delicious!

Add the sticker and colour in Paddington enjoying his favourite sandwich.

Jelly slide

Jonathan and Paddington have filled the paddling pool with gloopy jelly. Squelch!

Use your stickers to finish this messy jigsaw.

Wallpaper woes

Being a helpful bear is fun, but it can be very messy! And now Paddington is stuck to the wall!

Can you spot three differences between the two pictures?

All done? Stick a sticky paw here.

Answers: 1. A piece of wallpaper has changed colour, 2. There is a suitcase, 3. Jonathan is wearing a hat

Messy mishaps

Whoops! It looks like Paddington has made a bit of a mess.

Can you see what's under each splat? Add the correct sticker next to each picture.

Heatwave

When the weather is hot,
Paddington knows what to do.
He makes marmalade
ice cream!

Can you help Paddington spot these four things? Colour in an ice cream when you find each item.

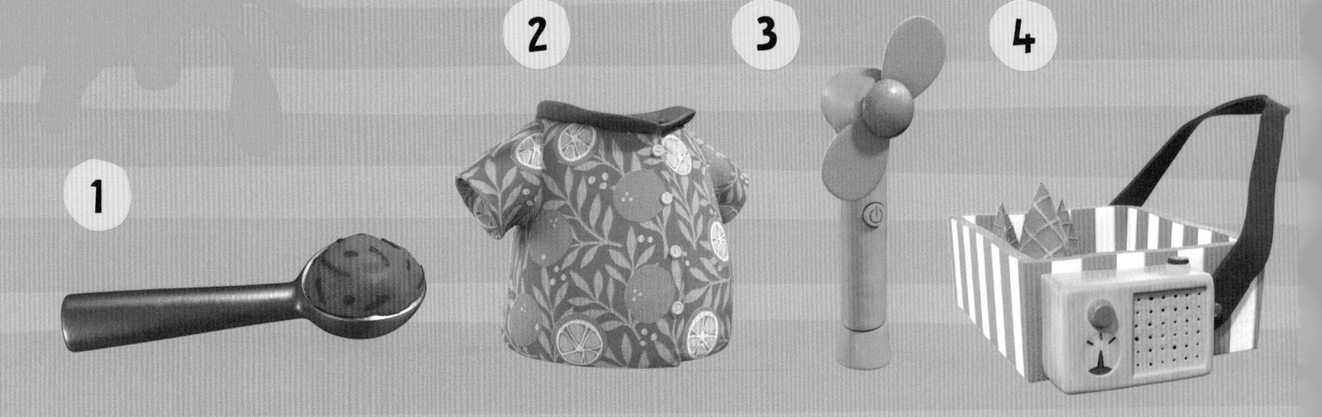

All done?
Stick a sticky
paw here.

Sticky stuff

Jonathan is playing a game of odd one out with Paddington.

Can you help by pointing to the odd one out in each row?

1

A

B

C

D

2

A

B

C

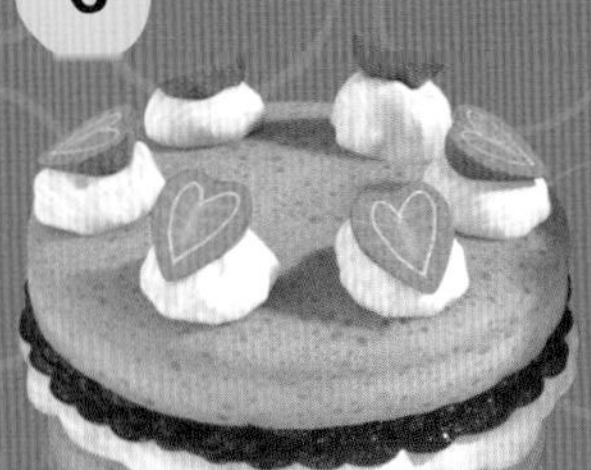

D

3

A

B

C

D

4

A

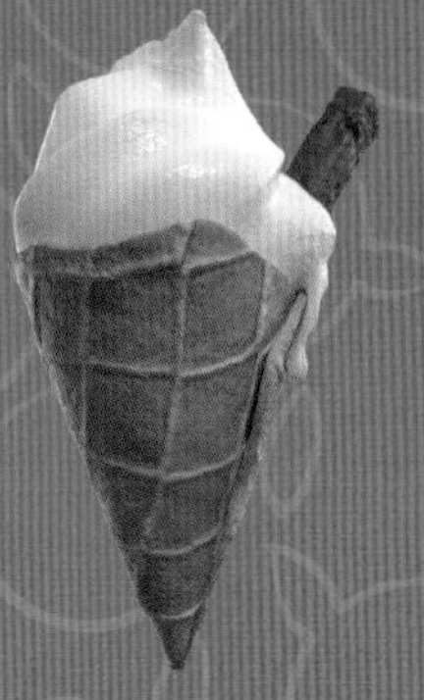

B

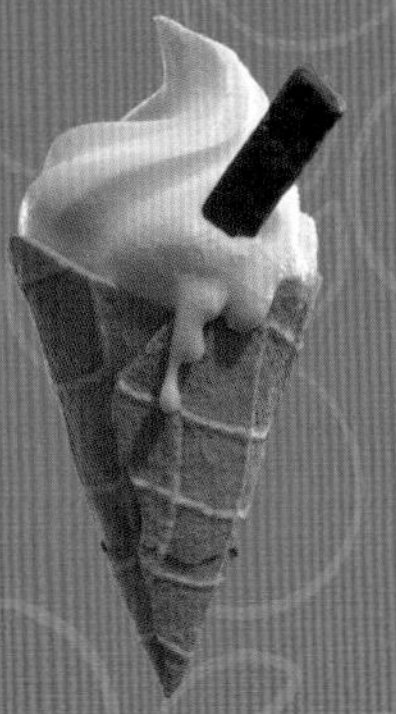

C

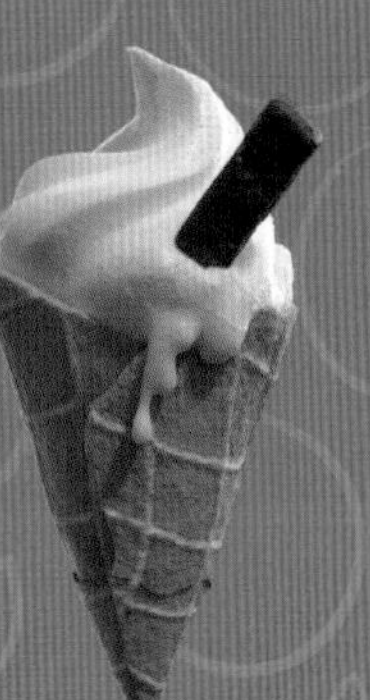

D

Answers: 1. C, 2. B, 3. D, 4. A

Marmalade maze

Oh dear! Paddington has lost his last jar of marmalade.

Use your finger to show this confused bear through the maze to find his marmalade.

Clue! Look for marmalade splats to show you the way.

Perfect picnic

Mr Brown has taken everybody to the park for a beautiful sunset picnic.

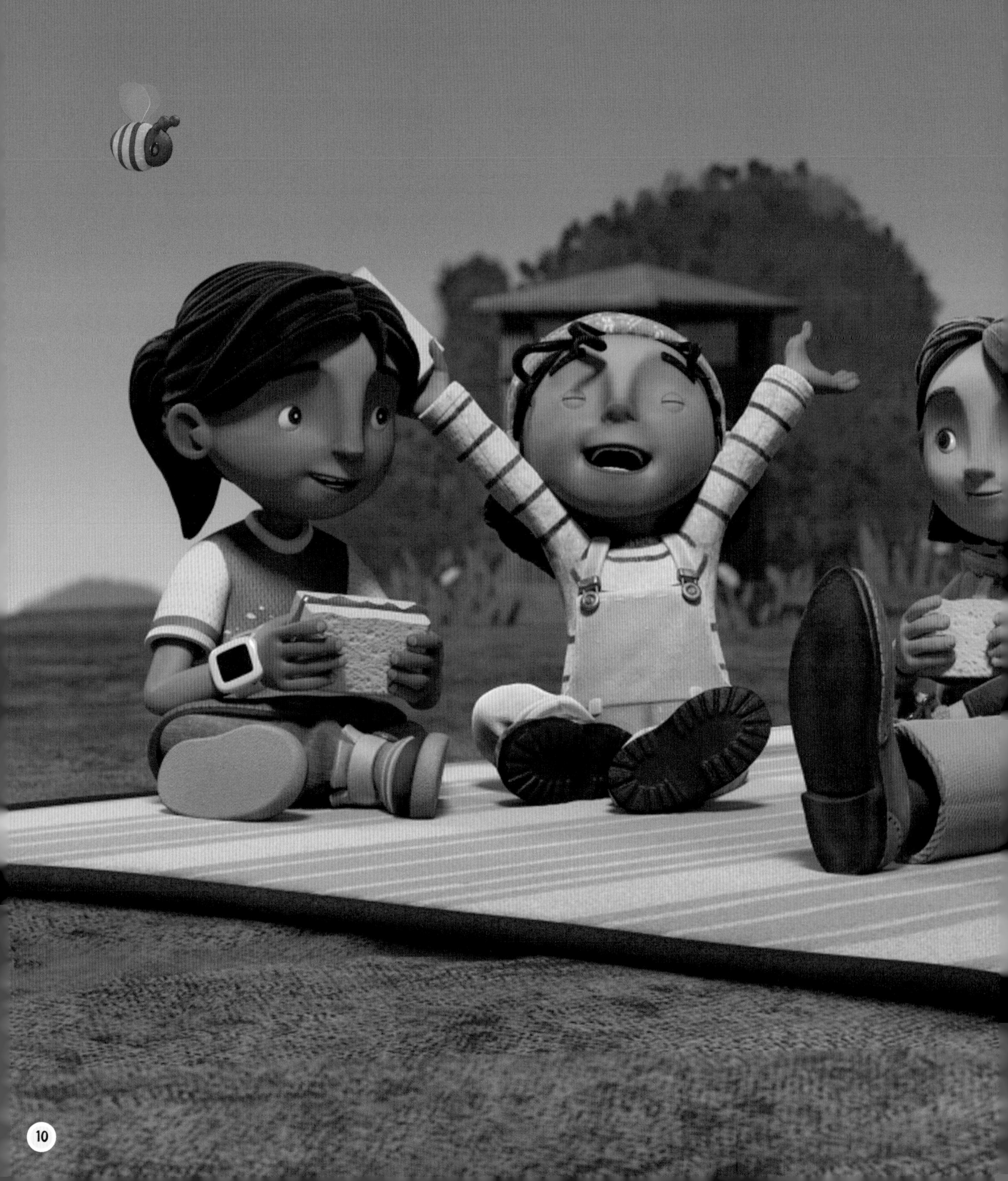

Use your stickers to give them all lots of sticky food.

Ready, set . . . paint!

Mrs Brown is an artist and Paddington is helping her do some very messy painting.

Stick on their paintbrushes and add paint splat stickers all over the room!

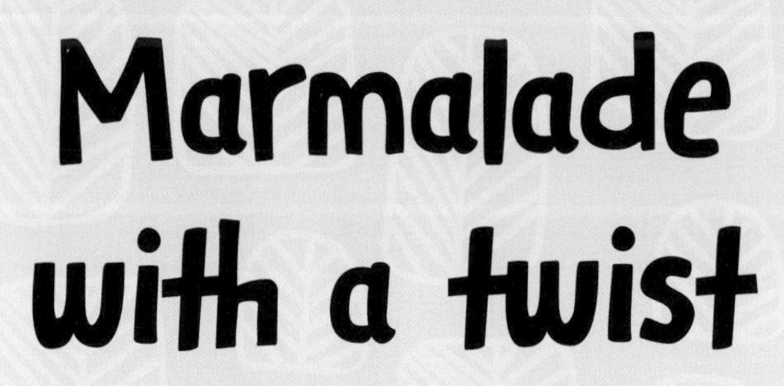

Marmalade with a twist

There's nothing that Paddington loves more than marmalade sandwiches. Today he's getting creative!

Draw your favourite fillings on this bread to invent your own marmalade sandwich.

Blackberry picking

The Browns are busy in the garden looking for juicy blackberries to bake with.

What comes next? Add a sticker to finish the sequence.

Add a sticker next to the biggest pile of berries.
1
2
3

Sweet treats

The sun is shining, so Paddington is cooling down with a tasty marmalade ice cream.

Can you colour in Paddington enjoying his ice cream?